MAD LIBS®

by Tris

MAD LIBS
An Imprint of Penguin Random House LLC, New York

Concept created by Roger Price & Leonard Stern

Published by Mad Libs,
an imprint of Penguin Random House LLC, New York.
Printed in the USA.

Visit us online at www.penguinrandomhouse.com.

ISBN 9780593223550
1 3 5 7 9 10 8 6 4 2

MAD LIBS®

INSTRUCTIONS

MAD LIBS® is a game for people who don't like games! It can be played by one, two, three, four, or forty.

• RIDICULOUSLY SIMPLE DIRECTIONS

In this tablet you will find stories containing blank spaces where words are left out. One player, the READER, selects one of these stories. The READER does not tell anyone what the story is about. Instead, he/she asks the other players, the WRITERS, to give him/her words. These words are used to fill in the blank spaces in the story.

• TO PLAY

The READER asks each WRITER in turn to call out a word—an adjective or a noun or whatever the space calls for—and uses them to fill in the blank spaces in the story. The result is a MAD LIBS® game.

When the READER then reads the completed MAD LIBS® game to the other players, they will discover that they have written a story that is fantastic, screamingly funny, shocking, silly, crazy, or just plain dumb—depending upon which words each WRITER called out.

• EXAMPLE (*Before* and *After*)

"________________ !" he said ________________
EXCLAMATION ADVERB

as he jumped into his convertible ________________ and
NOUN

drove off with his ________________ wife.
ADJECTIVE

"____OUCH____ !" he said ____HAPPILY____
EXCLAMATION ADVERB

as he jumped into his convertible ____CAT____ and
NOUN

drove off with his ____BRAVE____ wife.
ADJECTIVE

MAD LIBS®

QUICK REVIEW

In case you have forgotten what adjectives, adverbs, nouns, and verbs are, here is a quick review:

An ADJECTIVE describes something or somebody. *Lumpy*, *soft*, *ugly*, *messy*, and *short* are adjectives.

An ADVERB tells how something is done. It modifies a verb and usually ends in "ly." *Modestly*, *stupidly*, *greedily*, and *carefully* are adverbs.

A NOUN is the name of a person, place, or thing. *Sidewalk*, *umbrella*, *bridle*, *bathtub*, and *nose* are nouns.

A VERB is an action word. *Run*, *pitch*, *jump*, and *swim* are verbs. Put the verbs in past tense if the directions say PAST TENSE. *Ran*, *pitched*, *jumped*, and *swam* are verbs in the past tense.

When we ask for A PLACE, we mean any sort of place: a country or city (*Spain*, *Cleveland*) or a room (*bathroom*, *kitchen*).

An EXCLAMATION or SILLY WORD is any sort of funny sound, gasp, grunt, or outcry, like *Wow!*, *Ouch!*, *Whomp!*, *Ick!*, and *Gadzooks!*

When we ask for specific words, like a NUMBER, a COLOR, an ANIMAL, or a PART OF THE BODY, we mean a word that is one of those things, like *seven*, *blue*, *horse*, or *head*.

When we ask for a PLURAL, it means more than one. For example, *cat* pluralized is *cats*.

MAD LIBS® is fun to play with friends, but you can also play it by yourself! To begin with, DO NOT look at the story on the page below. Fill in the blanks on this page with the words called for. Then, using the words you have selected, fill in the blank spaces in the story.

Now you've created your own hilarious MAD LIBS® game!

BY THE POWER OF GRAYSKULL!

COLOR ____________________

NOUN ____________________

ADJECTIVE ____________________

PERSON IN ROOM ____________________

CELEBRITY ____________________

ADJECTIVE ____________________

OCCUPATION ____________________

NOUN ____________________

SAME NOUN ____________________

PART OF THE BODY ____________________

NOUN ____________________

NOUN ____________________

ADJECTIVE ____________________

ANIMAL ____________________

PERSON IN ROOM ____________________

SOMETHING ALIVE ____________________

ADJECTIVE ____________________

NOUN ____________________

MAD LIBS®
BY THE POWER OF GRAYSKULL!

"By the power of ____________ (COLOR) -skull!" When you hear those heroic words, you know you're about to enter the world of He-Man, the greatest ____________ (NOUN) in the universe! He-Man's ____________ (ADJECTIVE) identity is Prince Adam, the so-called cowardly son of King ____________ (PERSON IN ROOM) and Queen ____________ (CELEBRITY). Prince Adam lived a/an ____________ (ADJECTIVE) life in the Kingdom of Eternos on the planet Eternia until the ____________ (OCCUPATION) of Castle Grayskull gave him the ____________ (NOUN) of Power. Now, when Prince Adam holds the ____________ (SAME NOUN) over his ____________ (PART OF THE BODY) and says, "By the power of Gray-____________ (NOUN), I have the power!," magical bolts of ____________ (NOUN) transform him into the ____________ (ADJECTIVE) hero He-Man. Together with allies like Battle ____________ (ANIMAL), Teela, Orko, ____________ (PERSON IN ROOM) -At-Arms, and Ram ____________ (SOMETHING ALIVE), He-Man has sworn to use his powers to fight the ____________ (ADJECTIVE) Skeletor and keep the ____________ (NOUN) safe from the forces of evil!

MAD LIBS® is fun to play with friends, but you can also play it by yourself! To begin with, DO NOT look at the story on the page below. Fill in the blanks on this page with the words called for. Then, using the words you have selected, fill in the blank spaces in the story.

Now you've created your own hilarious MAD LIBS® game!

WE HAVE THE POWER

ADJECTIVE ____________________

ADVERB ____________________

ADJECTIVE ____________________

VERB ____________________

OCCUPATION ____________________

VEHICLE (PLURAL) ____________________

ADJECTIVE ____________________

PART OF THE BODY ____________________

NOUN ____________________

PART OF THE BODY (PLURAL) ____________________

VERB ____________________

NOUN ____________________

OCCUPATION ____________________

NOUN ____________________

PLURAL NOUN ____________________

NOUN ____________________

VERB ____________________

NOUN ____________________

MAD LIBS®

WE HAVE THE POWER

It's not easy battling someone as ________________ (ADJECTIVE) as Skeletor. ________________ (ADVERB), He-Man has a group of friends known as the ________________ (ADJECTIVE) Warriors to help him ________________ (VERB) the forces of evil. Man-At-Arms is the kingdom's ________________ (OCCUPATION) and built all the ________________ (VEHICLE (PLURAL)) that He-Man uses. He has a/an ________________ (ADJECTIVE) personality and a big mustache growing on his ________________ (PART OF THE BODY). Another ________________ (NOUN) who fights alongside He-Man is Man-E-________________ (PART OF THE BODY (PLURAL)). He has the power to ________________ (VERB) his face to look like a robot or a scary ________________ (NOUN). And then there's Orko, a/an ________________ (OCCUPATION) from the Timeless ________________ (NOUN). He can cast magical ________________ (PLURAL NOUN). Orko wears a red ________________ (NOUN) that hides his face in shadow, so his true appearance remains a mystery. These three, along with other Heroic Warriors like Teela and Battle Cat, have sworn to ________________ (VERB) at He-Man's side against Skeletor. Together, they are the Masters of the ________________ (NOUN)!

MAD LIBS® is fun to play with friends, but you can also play it by yourself! To begin with, DO NOT look at the story on the page below. Fill in the blanks on this page with the words called for. Then, using the words you have selected, fill in the blank spaces in the story.

Now you've created your own hilarious MAD LIBS® game!

TRAINING DAY

PART OF THE BODY (PLURAL) ____________

VERB ____________

SOMETHING ALIVE ____________

ADJECTIVE ____________

VERB ENDING IN "ING" ____________

PART OF THE BODY (PLURAL) ____________

NOUN ____________

SOMETHING ALIVE (PLURAL) ____________

NOUN ____________

ADVERB ____________

TYPE OF FOOD ____________

ADJECTIVE ____________

TYPE OF LIQUID ____________

NOUN ____________

NOUN ____________

VERB ____________

MAD LIBS®

TRAINING DAY

If you want to have powerful ______________ like He-Man to
PART OF THE BODY (PLURAL)

help you ______________ evil, then let ______________ -At-Arms
VERB / SOMETHING ALIVE

help you with these ______________ training tips:
ADJECTIVE

- ______________ to the top of Dragonmount is a great way
  VERB ENDING IN "ING"

  to build strong ______________, but be careful of the
  PART OF THE BODY (PLURAL)

  ______________ -breathing ______________ that live
  NOUN / SOMETHING ALIVE (PLURAL)

  there!

- Eating a healthy ______________ at every meal is important.
  NOUN

  ______________ journey to the top of Mount Zelite to find the rare
  ADVERB

  ______________ that grows there. It tastes ______________ when
  TYPE OF FOOD / ADJECTIVE

  dipped in ______________.
  TYPE OF LIQUID

- You may not have a/an ______________ Sword like He-Man, but
  NOUN

  you can use a/an ______________ instead. ______________ with it
  NOUN / VERB

  every day until you're skilled enough to use it in battle!

MAD LIBS® is fun to play with friends, but you can also play it by yourself! To begin with, DO NOT look at the story on the page below. Fill in the blanks on this page with the words called for. Then, using the words you have selected, fill in the blank spaces in the story.

Now you've created your own hilarious MAD LIBS® game!

ALL HAIL SKELETOR!

NOUN ____________________

ADJECTIVE ____________________

PART OF THE BODY ____________________

ADJECTIVE ____________________

NOUN ____________________

VERB ____________________

NOUN ____________________

OCCUPATION ____________________

PLURAL NOUN ____________________

VERB ____________________

NOUN ____________________

SILLY WORD ____________________

SAME OCCUPATION ____________________

PART OF THE BODY ____________________

NOUN ____________________

PART OF THE BODY ____________________

A PLACE ____________________

ADJECTIVE ____________________

MAD LIBS®

ALL HAIL SKELETOR!

Skeletor, Lord of ____________ (NOUN), here! How unpleasant it is to meet such a/an ____________ (ADJECTIVE) He-Man fan such as yourself. Nothing rattles my ____________ (PART OF THE BODY) more than He-Man always acting so ____________ (ADJECTIVE), but we all know that he's really a sniveling ____________ (NOUN). I have but one goal in life . . . to ____________ (VERB) He-Man out of existence with my Havoc ____________ (NOUN) and become the ____________ (OCCUPATION) of Eternia! With He-Man out of the way, the ____________ (PLURAL NOUN) of Castle Grayskull will finally be mine, and He-Man's so-called "Heroic Warriors" will ____________ (VERB) before me as their new ____________ (NOUN) and shout, " ____________ (SILLY WORD), Skeletor! The greatest ____________ (SAME OCCUPATION) to rule Eternia!" Oh, the things I'll do once I rule . . . but first I'll make Man-At-Arms shave his ____________ (PART OF THE BODY). Then I'll take off Orko's ____________ (NOUN) so I can finally see what his ____________ (PART OF THE BODY) looks like. Of course, someone as awesome as me deserves to be the ruler of (the) ____________ (A PLACE). And that includes the ____________ (ADJECTIVE) little planet where you live! Hahahahahaha!

MAD LIBS® is fun to play with friends, but you can also play it by yourself! To begin with, DO NOT look at the story on the page below. Fill in the blanks on this page with the words called for. Then, using the words you have selected, fill in the blank spaces in the story.

Now you've created your own hilarious MAD LIBS® game!

YOUR TOUR OF CASTLE GRAYSKULL

PART OF THE BODY ________________

PLURAL NOUN ________________

ADJECTIVE ________________

ADJECTIVE ________________

A PLACE ________________

NOUN ________________

NOUN ________________

SOMETHING ALIVE (PLURAL) ________________

NUMBER ________________

A PLACE ________________

NOUN ________________

PART OF THE BODY (PLURAL) ________________

NOUN ________________

PLURAL NOUN ________________

TYPE OF BUILDING ________________

NOUN ________________

MAD LIBS®

YOUR TOUR OF CASTLE GRAYSKULL

When you first arrive at Castle Grayskull, you'll notice the castle looks like a giant ______________ (PART OF THE BODY) carved from gray ______________ (PLURAL NOUN). But don't let this ______________ (ADJECTIVE) appearance fool you. Castle Grayskull is the ______________ (ADJECTIVE) home to me, the Sorceress of (the) ______________ (A PLACE), and is a safe place for He-______________ (NOUN). Legend has it, the castle protects an ancient and mysterious ______________ (NOUN) from those who would misuse it, like Skeletor or the Snake ______________ (SOMETHING ALIVE (PLURAL)). Castle Grayskull was built over ______________ (NUMBER) years ago on the edge of the Evergreen ______________ (A PLACE) and is surrounded by a bottomless ______________ (NOUN). You enter the castle through the Jaw Bridge, which is filled with huge ______________ (PART OF THE BODY (PLURAL)). Castle Grayskull also has a Hall of ______________ (NOUN) and a Portal Chamber, which is filled with magical ______________ (PLURAL NOUN) that can teleport you anywhere on Eternia. Although the inside may look like a normal ______________ (TYPE OF BUILDING), there's one thing this castle has that others never will . . . the Power of ______________ (NOUN)!

MAD LIBS® is fun to play with friends, but you can also play it by yourself! To begin with, DO NOT look at the story on the page below. Fill in the blanks on this page with the words called for. Then, using the words you have selected, fill in the blank spaces in the story.

Now you've created your own hilarious MAD LIBS® game!

A COWARDLY ROAR

NUMBER ____________

ADVERB ____________

ANIMAL ____________

SILLY WORD ____________

PART OF THE BODY ____________

ADJECTIVE ____________

NOUN ____________

ANIMAL ____________

PART OF THE BODY ____________

ARTICLE OF CLOTHING ____________

SAME ANIMAL ____________

ADJECTIVE ____________

NOUN ____________

VERB ____________

EXCLAMATION ____________

VERB ENDING IN "ING" ____________

ANIMAL ____________

TYPE OF FOOD ____________

MAD LIBS®

A COWARDLY ROAR

_______________ years ago, when I was just a kitten, Prince Adam
NUMBER

_____________ saved me from a saber-toothed _____________ in the
ADVERB ANIMAL

_________________ Jungle. After Prince Adam brought me to
SILLY WORD

Eternos, Teela named me "Cringer" because I'm afraid of my own

_____________. Life with Prince Adam was very _____________,
PART OF THE BODY ADJECTIVE

but then he had to go and use his Power _____________ to turn me
NOUN

into—*ohhhh*—Battle _________________. Oh, gosh, when he does
ANIMAL

that, my ______________________ doubles in size, and I wear a red
PART OF THE BODY

______________________ and saddle so He-Man can ride me into
ARTICLE OF CLOTHING

battle. As that brute Battle _____________, I have a/an _____________
SAME ANIMAL ADJECTIVE

roar. But when I'm Cringer, I want to hide every time He-Man raises

his _____________. I want to help He-Man, but I _____________
NOUN VERB

when I think of—___________________!—___________________
EXCLAMATION VERB ENDING IN "ING"

with Skeletor! Sigh. I wish He-Man would turn me into a cute

______________ instead so I could just lie around Castle Grayskull
ANIMAL

and eat ____________.
TYPE OF FOOD

MAD LIBS® is fun to play with friends, but you can also play it by yourself! To begin with, DO NOT look at the story on the page below. Fill in the blanks on this page with the words called for. Then, using the words you have selected, fill in the blank spaces in the story.

Now you've created your own hilarious MAD LIBS® game!

MAN OF MAN-E-TALENTS

PART OF THE BODY (PLURAL) ____________

ADVERB ____________

ADJECTIVE ____________

SAME PART OF THE BODY ____________

SOMETHING ALIVE ____________

SOMETHING ALIVE (PLURAL) ____________

ADVERB ____________

EXCLAMATION ____________

VERB ____________

OCCUPATION ____________

A PLACE ____________

VERB ____________

EXCLAMATION ____________

VERB ENDING IN "ING" ____________

ADJECTIVE ____________

CELEBRITY ____________

PART OF THE BODY ____________

NOUN ____________

MAD LIBS®

PROTECT YOUR SECRET IDENTITY

If you have a secret identity as the most ____________ (ADJECTIVE) person in (the) ____________ (A PLACE), here are some of Prince Adam's ____________ (ADJECTIVE) tips on how you can keep it a secret!

- Only reveal your true identity to a/an ____________ (ADJECTIVE) group of ____________ (PLURAL NOUN) that you can trust. The fewer ____________ (SAME PLURAL NOUN) who know you're really ____________ (CELEBRITY), the better!
- If you use a magic ____________ (NOUN) to transform, never do it in a place where people can ____________ (VERB) you.
- Make sure you wear a/an ____________ (ADJECTIVE) ____________ (ARTICLE OF CLOTHING) that helps hide your true identity.
- Always have a/an ____________ (ADJECTIVE) excuse when your ____________ (OCCUPATION (PLURAL)) ask where you were. Saying you had to ____________ (ADVERB) go to (the) ____________ (A PLACE) is always a good one.

MAD LIBS® is fun to play with friends, but you can also play it by yourself! To begin with, DO NOT look at the story on the page below. Fill in the blanks on this page with the words called for. Then, using the words you have selected, fill in the blank spaces in the story.

Now you've created your own hilarious MAD LIBS® game!

POWER OF THE SEA!

VERB ____________

SOMETHING ALIVE ____________

VERB ____________

PLURAL NOUN ____________

PART OF THE BODY (PLURAL) ____________

VERB ____________

ADVERB ____________

PART OF THE BODY ____________

ANIMAL (PLURAL) ____________

VERB ____________

VERB ENDING IN "ING" ____________

TYPE OF LIQUID ____________

NOUN ____________

ADJECTIVE ____________

ANIMAL ____________

PART OF THE BODY ____________

SILLY WORD ____________

NOUN ____________

MAD LIBS®

POWER OF THE SEA!

When it comes to power, who's the only one of Skeletor's Evil Warriors who can ____________ (VERB) underwater? It's me, Mer-Man, because I'm part fish and part ____________ (SOMETHING ALIVE)! That means I can live and ____________ (VERB) above and below the ocean waves. I have ____________ (PLURAL NOUN) on the sides of my head, and webbed ____________ (PART OF THE BODY (PLURAL)) and hands that allow me to ____________ (VERB) fast. But being able to swim and breathe underwater ____________ (ADVERB) isn't my only skill. I can also use my ____________ (PART OF THE BODY) to control ____________ (ANIMAL (PLURAL)) and make them do my bidding. I'm super strong, but even though I can ____________ (VERB) on land, my strength is even greater when I'm ____________ (VERB ENDING IN "ING") in ____________ (TYPE OF LIQUID). I also possess a powerful sword that can blast a ray to encase He-Man in ____________ (NOUN). Sure, Skeletor may call me ____________ (ADJECTIVE) names like ____________ (ANIMAL)-face or fin-____________ (PART OF THE BODY), or even ____________ (SILLY WORD), but I know deep in his bony ____________ (NOUN), he really loves me!

MAD LIBS® is fun to play with friends, but you can also play it by yourself! To begin with, DO NOT look at the story on the page below. Fill in the blanks on this page with the words called for. Then, using the words you have selected, fill in the blank spaces in the story.

Now you've created your own hilarious MAD LIBS® game!

A MIND FOR EVIL

PART OF THE BODY ________________

ADJECTIVE ________________

ADVERB ________________

EXCLAMATION ________________

PART OF THE BODY ________________

NOUN ________________

VERB ________________

ADVERB ________________

NOUN ________________

PLURAL NOUN ________________

OCCUPATION ________________

ADJECTIVE ________________

PART OF THE BODY (PLURAL) ________________

PART OF THE BODY ________________

CELEBRITY ________________

MAD LIBS®

A MIND FOR EVIL

Are you worried that your ________________ is being controlled by
PART OF THE BODY

Beast Man? Here are a few ________________ signs to look for:
ADJECTIVE

- Do you get the sudden urge to ________________ yell,
ADVERB

"________________! Get He-Man!"?
EXCLAMATION

- Does your ________________ twitch as you hear Beast Man's
PART OF THE BODY

________________ in your head?
NOUN

- Do you have a desire to ________________ Castle Grayskull and try
VERB

to ________________ steal the mysterious ________________ that's
ADVERB / NOUN

hidden inside?

- Do you want to give all your ________________ to Skeletor and
PLURAL NOUN

forever swear that he is your ________________?
OCCUPATION

If you're experiencing any of these ________________ symptoms,
ADJECTIVE

call Man-At-________________ at once, because your
PART OF THE BODY (PLURAL)

________________ is definitely being controlled by ________________!
PART OF THE BODY / CELEBRITY

MAD LIBS® is fun to play with friends, but you can also play it by yourself! To begin with, DO NOT look at the story on the page below. Fill in the blanks on this page with the words called for. Then, using the words you have selected, fill in the blank spaces in the story.

Now you've created your own hilarious MAD LIBS® game!

TROLLA-LA ALL THE WAY HOME

ADJECTIVE ____________________

NOUN ____________________

ADJECTIVE ____________________

VERB ____________________

VERB ____________________

TYPE OF LIQUID ____________________

NUMBER ____________________

OCCUPATION (PLURAL) ____________________

ADJECTIVE ____________________

OCCUPATION ____________________

SILLY WORD ____________________

PLURAL NOUN ____________________

NOUN ____________________

NOUN ____________________

VERB (PAST TENSE) ____________________

VERB ____________________

VERB ENDING IN "ING" ____________________

A PLACE ____________________

MAD LIBS®

TROLLA-LA ALL THE WAY HOME

It's Orko, here to tell you some ____________ (ADJECTIVE) things about my home ____________ (NOUN), Trolla. Things on Trolla are very ____________ (ADJECTIVE) compared to life on Eternia. For example, trees ____________ (VERB) upside down. Instead of swimming, fish ____________ (VERB) in the air. Instead of flying, birds swim in ____________ (TYPE OF LIQUID)! Trolla is ruled by ____________ (NUMBER) elderly Trollans known as the Crimson ____________ (OCCUPATION (PLURAL)). And we also have a noble and ____________ (ADJECTIVE) ____________ (OCCUPATION) named the High ____________ (SILLY WORD). Back on Trolla, I'm considered one of the greatest ____________ (PLURAL NOUN) on the planet, but after a cosmic ____________ (NOUN) brought me to Eternia, I lost my magic ____________ (NOUN) when I ____________ (VERB (PAST TENSE)) with a tree. Since then, things don't always work out so well when I ____________ (VERB) a spell. I love Eternia, but I do miss Trolla, and so I like to go back and visit when I'm not ____________ (VERB ENDING IN "ING") He-Man to keep (the) ____________ (A PLACE) safe from that no-good Skeletor.

MAD LIBS® is fun to play with friends, but you can also play it by yourself! To begin with, DO NOT look at the story on the page below. Fill in the blanks on this page with the words called for. Then, using the words you have selected, fill in the blank spaces in the story.

Now you've created your own hilarious MAD LIBS® game!

WHAT'S IN A NAME?

NOUN ____________________

ADJECTIVE ____________________

PART OF THE BODY (PLURAL) ____________________

SOMETHING ALIVE (PLURAL) ____________________

NOUN ____________________

ADJECTIVE ____________________

SOMETHING ALIVE ____________________

ADJECTIVE ____________________

ANIMAL ____________________

OCCUPATION ____________________

VERB ____________________

SILLY WORD ____________________

PLURAL NOUN ____________________

ADJECTIVE ____________________

NOUN ____________________

NOUN ____________________

ADJECTIVE ____________________

MAD LIBS®

WHAT'S IN A NAME?

Skeleton: Beast Man, you flea-bitten fur-____________ (NOUN)! I need a/an ____________ (ADJECTIVE) name to strike fear into the ____________ (PART OF THE BODY (PLURAL)) of the ____________ (SOMETHING ALIVE (PLURAL)) of Eternia. What do you think of "Skeletor: the King of ____________ (NOUN)"?

Beast Man: That sounds too ____________ (ADJECTIVE). Maybe something like "Skeletor: the ____________ (SOMETHING ALIVE) of Scariness"!

Skeletor: That would be ____________ (ADJECTIVE) if I were a dim-witted ____________ (ANIMAL) such as yourself. I am the ____________ (OCCUPATION) of Eternia! People must see me and ____________ (VERB) in fear!

Beast Man: How about "the ____________ (SILLY WORD) of Chaos"?

Skeletor: Why do I surround myself with such ____________ (PLURAL NOUN)? If I wanted a/an ____________ (ADJECTIVE) idea, I would've asked Mer-____________ (NOUN) for help! From now on, I shall be "Skeletor: the Lord of ____________ (NOUN)"!

Beast Man: Perfect. That's the most ____________ (ADJECTIVE) name of all!

MAD LIBS® is fun to play with friends, but you can also play it by yourself! To begin with, DO NOT look at the story on the page below. Fill in the blanks on this page with the words called for. Then, using the words you have selected, fill in the blank spaces in the story.

Now you've created your own hilarious MAD LIBS® game!

THE PLOT THICKENS

ADJECTIVE ______
A PLACE ______
NOUN ______
OCCUPATION ______
TYPE OF LIQUID ______
SOMETHING ALIVE ______
ADVERB ______
NOUN ______
SOMETHING ALIVE (PLURAL) ______
PART OF THE BODY ______
VERB ______
NOUN ______
VERB ______
NOUN ______
NOUN ______
SAME OCCUPATION ______
TYPE OF BUILDING ______
VERB (PAST TENSE) ______

MAD LIBS®

THE PLOT THICKENS

Skeletor has tried many ____________ (ADJECTIVE) plots to defeat He-Man and take over (the) ____________ (A PLACE). But his best one was when he used a/an ____________ (NOUN) ray to send He-Man and the ____________ (OCCUPATION) of Grayskull to a different dimension that was filled with nothing but ____________ (TYPE OF LIQUID) -spewing volcanoes. With the heroes gone, the ____________ (SOMETHING ALIVE) of Castle Grayskull ____________ (ADVERB) chose me, Teela, Captain of the Royal ____________ (NOUN), to defend the castle from Skeletor and his evil ____________ (SOMETHING ALIVE (PLURAL)). First, I defeated Trap ____________ (PART OF THE BODY) by making him ____________ (VERB) into a pit. Next, I tied up Evil-Lyn with a/an ____________ (NOUN). But when I tried to ____________ (VERB) Skeletor, he used his Havoc ____________ (NOUN) to stop me. Luckily, He-Man used his ____________ (NOUN) of Power to bring the ____________ (SAME OCCUPATION) of Grayskull and himself back to ____________ (TYPE OF BUILDING) Grayskull. Together, we ____________ (VERB (PAST TENSE)) Skeletor and saved Eternos!

MAD LIBS® is fun to play with friends, but you can also play it by yourself! To begin with, DO NOT look at the story on the page below. Fill in the blanks on this page with the words called for. Then, using the words you have selected, fill in the blank spaces in the story.

Now you've created your own hilarious MAD LIBS® game!

POWERED UP

ADJECTIVE ____________________

COLOR ____________________

PART OF THE BODY ____________________

ADVERB ____________________

ADJECTIVE ____________________

SAME COLOR ____________________

NOUN ____________________

OCCUPATION ____________________

NOUN ____________________

VERB ____________________

NOUN ____________________

SAME OCCUPATION ____________________

ANIMAL ____________________

VERB ____________________

VERB ____________________

PART OF THE BODY ____________________

ADJECTIVE ____________________

VERB ____________________

MAD LIBS®

POWERED UP

A long time ago, I lived a/an ____________ life as Prince Adam. Then
ADJECTIVE

the Sorceress of ____________ -skull gave me the Power Sword. By
COLOR

holding the sword over my ____________ and ____________
PART OF THE BODY ADVERB

repeating the ____________ phrase "By the power of
ADJECTIVE

____________ -skull, I have the ____________!," magical energy
SAME COLOR NOUN

strikes me, transforming me into ____________ -Man . . . the most
OCCUPATION

powerful ____________ in the universe. When I want to turn back
NOUN

into Prince Adam, I just ____________ the Power Sword over my
VERB

head and say, "Let the ____________ return!" Besides turning me
NOUN

into ____________ -Man, I can use the sword to turn my trusty
SAME OCCUPATION

pet ____________, Cringer, into ____________ Cat! The Power
ANIMAL VERB

Sword also allows me to ____________ Castle Grayskull. I just
VERB

hold the sword up and say, "By the power of Grayskull, I command

the ____________ Bridge to open!" Nothing in the universe is
PART OF THE BODY

more ____________ than my Power Sword, which explains why
ADJECTIVE

Skeletor is always trying to ____________ it.
VERB

MAD LIBS® is fun to play with friends, but you can also play it by yourself! To begin with, DO NOT look at the story on the page below. Fill in the blanks on this page with the words called for. Then, using the words you have selected, fill in the blank spaces in the story.

Now you've created your own hilarious MAD LIBS® game!

AIR MALE

ANIMAL ____________

OCCUPATION ____________

SAME ANIMAL ____________

VERB ____________

NOUN ____________

PLURAL NOUN ____________

PART OF THE BODY ____________

VERB ENDING IN "ING" ____________

VERB (PAST TENSE) ____________

NOUN ____________

ANIMAL ____________

SAME NOUN ____________

PERSON IN ROOM ____________

ADVERB ____________

VERB (PAST TENSE) ____________

VERB ____________

EXCLAMATION ____________

VEHICLE ____________

MAD LIBS®

WHAT EVIL-LYN REALLY WANTS

When it comes to evil ________________ (OCCUPATION (PLURAL)), everyone on Eternia knows there's no one more ____________ (ADJECTIVE) than I, Evil-Lyn! Skeletor likes to call me his "right ____________ (PART OF THE BODY) of evil," but I prefer to be called the __________ (ADJECTIVE) Queen of Evil, because one day I shall be the ruler of (the) ____________ (A PLACE)! Skeletor may be more ____________ (ADJECTIVE) than me now, but one day I'll use my magical ________________ (PLURAL NOUN) to take his power. Then I shall become the ____________ (NOUN) of all Eternia! Once I am, the first thing I'll do is ______________ (ADVERB) banish Beast ____________ (NOUN), Mer-________________ (PERSON IN ROOM), and ____________ (NOUN) Jaw. Those ______________ (ADJECTIVE) fools have caused me nothing but trouble! Then I shall make Snake Mountain my new ________________ (TYPE OF BUILDING), and from there I shall rule the planet. Of course, I'll still keep Skeletor around, since I'll be needing a new ____________ (OCCUPATION) to help me rule, but at the first sign of trouble, I'll make ______________________ (COLOR) ______________ (PLURAL NOUN) grow on his ______________ (PART OF THE BODY)!

MAD LIBS® is fun to play with friends, but you can also play it by yourself! To begin with, DO NOT look at the story on the page below. Fill in the blanks on this page with the words called for. Then, using the words you have selected, fill in the blank spaces in the story.

Now you've created your own hilarious MAD LIBS® game!

WELCOME TO ETERNIA

ADJECTIVE ____________

COLOR ____________

PART OF THE BODY ____________

NOUN ____________

SOMETHING ALIVE (PLURAL) ____________

ADJECTIVE ____________

PLURAL NOUN ____________

OCCUPATION ____________

VERB ENDING IN "ING" ____________

ADVERB ____________

VERB ____________

NOUN ____________

TYPE OF LIQUID ____________

SILLY WORD ____________

PLURAL NOUN ____________

PLURAL NOUN ____________

A PLACE ____________

MAD LIBS

WELCOME TO ETERNIA

Come visit Eternia, the most ____________ planet in the universe,
ADJECTIVE
with tourist sites for every traveler, including . . .

- **Castle** ____________ - ____________**:** the source of all ____________ in Eternia
COLOR / PART OF THE BODY / NOUN
- **Widget Fortress:** home of the ____________, a/an ____________ civilization that mines ____________ from underground caves
SOMETHING ALIVE (PLURAL) / ADJECTIVE / PLURAL NOUN
- **The** ____________ **Mountains:** home to the Bird People
OCCUPATION
- **Caves of the** ____________ **Crystals:** ____________ touch the crystals and listen to them ____________
VERB ENDING IN "ING" / ADVERB / VERB
- **The Valley of** ____________**:** a valley with streams of ____________ containing magical ____________
NOUN / TYPE OF LIQUID / SILLY WORD
- **If you're daring, visit the** ____________ **of Perpetua or the Demon Zone:** home to a race of evil ____________
PLURAL NOUN / PLURAL NOUN

There's something for everyone in (the) ____________!
A PLACE

MAD LIBS® is fun to play with friends, but you can also play it by yourself! To begin with, DO NOT look at the story on the page below. Fill in the blanks on this page with the words called for. Then, using the words you have selected, fill in the blank spaces in the story.

Now you've created your own hilarious MAD LIBS® game!

WHAT WOULD BEAST MAN DO?

ADJECTIVE ________________

VERB ________________

ADJECTIVE ________________

PART OF THE BODY ________________

PART OF THE BODY ________________

PLURAL NOUN ________________

ADVERB ________________

SOMETHING ALIVE ________________

NOUN ________________

SILLY WORD ________________

OCCUPATION ________________

NUMBER ________________

TYPE OF BUILDING ________________

VERB ________________

VERB ________________

SOMETHING ALIVE ________________

MAD LIBS®

WHAT WOULD BEAST MAN DO?

Rrrrrrr! Take this ______________ quiz to see if you can handle a
ADJECTIVE
battle the way Beast Man would.

1. If you want to help Skeletor ____________ He-Man in a battle,
VERB
you should: (a) Show He-Man the ____________ ____________
ADJECTIVE PART OF THE BODY
in your mouth and growl. (b) Use your ____________ control
PART OF THE BODY
powers to make Man-E- ____________ attack He-Man.
PLURAL NOUN
(c) ____________ run to the ____________ Jungle
ADVERB SOMETHING ALIVE
and hide.

2. If He-Man tries to use his ____________ Sword, you should: (a)
NOUN
Shout ____________ and run away. (b) Call Mer- ____________
SILLY WORD OCCUPATION
and ____________ Bad to help you. (c) Climb to the top of
NUMBER
____________ Grayskull and ____________ at the moon.
TYPE OF BUILDING VERB

If you guessed *b* for both questions, then congratulations. You
____________ just like ____________ Man!
VERB SOMETHING ALIVE

MAD LIBS® is fun to play with friends, but you can also play it by yourself! To begin with, DO NOT look at the story on the page below. Fill in the blanks on this page with the words called for. Then, using the words you have selected, fill in the blank spaces in the story.

Now you've created your own hilarious MAD LIBS® game!

VEHICLES OF ETERNIA

TYPE OF LIQUID ____________________

ADJECTIVE ____________________

PART OF THE BODY (PLURAL) ____________________

NOUN ____________________

PLURAL NOUN ____________________

VERB ____________________

VEHICLE ____________________

ADJECTIVE ____________________

NOUN ____________________

VERB ____________________

NOUN ____________________

ADVERB ____________________

A PLACE ____________________

COLOR ____________________

ANIMAL ____________________

NOUN ____________________

MAD LIBS®

VEHICLES OF ETERNIA

Land, ______________ (TYPE OF LIQUID), or air, here's a list of ______________ (ADJECTIVE) vehicles Man-At-______________ (PART OF THE BODY (PLURAL)) has made to help fight Skeletor:

- The Attak ______________ (NOUN) is a tank-like vehicle with ______________ (PLURAL NOUN) instead of wheels, so it can ______________ (VERB) over any terrain.
- The Wind Raider is a jet-propelled ______________ (VEHICLE) equipped with ______________ (ADJECTIVE) lasers for battle!
- The Battle ______________ (NOUN) is powerful enough to ______________ (VERB) a mountain! The front detaches to become a flying ______________ (NOUN) that can ______________ (ADVERB) soar through (the) ______________ (A PLACE).
- The Bashasaurus is a/an ______________ (COLOR) vehicle that looks like a prehistoric ______________ (ANIMAL). Its huge ______________ (NOUN) can bash anything that gets in its way!

MAD LIBS® is fun to play with friends, but you can also play it by yourself! To begin with, DO NOT look at the story on the page below. Fill in the blanks on this page with the words called for. Then, using the words you have selected, fill in the blank spaces in the story.

Now you've created your own hilarious MAD LIBS® game!

SKELETOR'S OTHER HENCHMEN

NOUN ______________________

PART OF THE BODY ______________________

ADJECTIVE ______________________

VERB ______________________

LAST NAME ______________________

PART OF THE BODY (PLURAL) ______________________

TYPE OF LIQUID ______________________

ADJECTIVE ______________________

PART OF THE BODY ______________________

VERB ______________________

ADJECTIVE ______________________

NOUN ______________________

EXCLAMATION ______________________

PLURAL NOUN ______________________

NUMBER ______________________

PART OF THE BODY (PLURAL) ______________________

ADJECTIVE ______________________

NOUN ______________________

MAD LIBS®

SKELETOR'S OTHER HENCHMEN

So that muscle-bound ____________ (NOUN), He-Man, thinks he'll stop me, Skeletor, from taking over Castle Gray-____________ (PART OF THE BODY)!? Let's see which of my ____________ (ADJECTIVE) Warriors will help me ____________ (VERB) He-Man once and for all! Perhaps I'll call on Kobra ____________ (LAST NAME). He'll be able to stretch his ____________ (PART OF THE BODY (PLURAL)), capture He-Man, and spray him with ____________ (TYPE OF LIQUID) mist! But Clawful could crush He-Man with his ____________ (ADJECTIVE) ____________ (PART OF THE BODY). If I really want to ____________ (VERB) things up, there's always Stinkor, the ____________ (ADJECTIVE) Master of ____________ (NOUN). One smell of him and He-Man will cry, "____________ (EXCLAMATION)!" and beg for ____________ (PLURAL NOUN)! Of course, Tri-Klops's ____________ (NUMBER) ____________ (PART OF THE BODY (PLURAL)) make him a match for anyone! So many choices, but . . . who am I kidding . . . they're just a bunch of ____________ (ADJECTIVE) fools who couldn't beat He-Man even if they had the most powerful ____________ (NOUN) in the universe.

MAD LIBS® is fun to play with friends, but you can also play it by yourself! To begin with, DO NOT look at the story on the page below. Fill in the blanks on this page with the words called for. Then, using the words you have selected, fill in the blank spaces in the story.

Now you've created your own hilarious MAD LIBS® game!

A HE-MANLY RECAP

NOUN ____________

NOUN ____________

ADJECTIVE ____________

VERB ____________

SOMETHING ALIVE (PLURAL) ____________

PART OF THE BODY ____________

VERB ____________

PLURAL NOUN ____________

ADJECTIVE ____________

PLURAL NOUN ____________

ADJECTIVE ____________

NOUN ____________

ADJECTIVE ____________

NOUN ____________

ANIMAL ____________

NOUN ____________

MAD LIBS

A HE-MANLY RECAP

You don't need to have a/an ________________ (NOUN) Sword or be a/an ____________ (NOUN) of the Universe, like me, He-Man, to do good. The power to be _____________ (ADJECTIVE) is inside all of us. All it takes is a desire to _______________ (VERB) any _____________________ (SOMETHING ALIVE (PLURAL)) who need help. When you help someone, you bring a smile to their _____________ (PART OF THE BODY) and make them want to ____________ (VERB) others, too. That's why I use my _________________ (PLURAL NOUN) to make the world a better place! Too bad Skeletor is always acting ____________ (ADJECTIVE) and putting his own selfish needs first instead of helping ______________ (PLURAL NOUN). Living like that will only make ____________ (ADJECTIVE) things happen, and then no one will want to be your _____________ (NOUN). That's why Skeletor's so ____________ (ADJECTIVE) and lives on a rocky ____________ (NOUN) that looks like a/an ___________ (ANIMAL). Until next time, remember: By the power of Grayskull . . . you have the ____________ (NOUN), too!

MAD LIBS®

Download on the
App Store

GET IT ON
Google Play